EDGES

Swift Encounter

Book 1

Bjorn Esterday Was Not Born Yesterday

Wynter Sommers

GJ dePillis

USA Copyright © 2017 Susan E dePillis & GJ dePillis

TXu001885818
PAu 3-627-478, 1-798104171, PAu003401882, PAu003759141,
1-787-353831
Library of Congress Control Number: 2019930919

Published by Pure Force Enterprises, Inc.
California, USA
Since 2002

ISBN-13: 978-1-7184-0002-3
ISBN-10: 1-7184-0002-0

DEDICATION

To all of us whose hearts reach out to change the world around, whose minds calculate the next strategic move, whose souls crave adventure and value freedom of democracy. To the spirit harnessing the power of fiction to alter our reality, making the world a better place for everyone.

Bjorn Esterday Was Not Born Yesterday Series

Firebrand (9 Stories +Conversation Station Book)
Edges (9 Stories +Conversation Station Book)
Gone (18 Stories + 2 Conversation Station Books)

Bjorn EDGES Series
EDGES Book 1-Swift Encounter
EDGES Book 2-Rousing Attack
EDGES Book 3-One Foot Under
EDGES Book 4-Earthshake
EDGES Book 5-Broken String
EDGES Book 6-Key Witness
EDGES Book 7-Who is She?
EDGES Book 8-Vanish
EDGES Book 9-Chase or Die

Bjorn Series Alternate Reading Plan

1st   Edges Book 1
2nd   Edges Book 2
3rd   Gone Book 1
4th   Firebrand Book 1
5th   Edges Book 3
6th   Firebrand Book 2
7th   Gone Book 2
8th   Gone Book 3
9th   Firebrand Book 3
10th Gone Book 4
11th Firebrand Book 4
12th Gone Book 5
13th Gone Book 6
14th Edges Book 4
15th Firebrand Book 5
16th Gone Book 7
17th Firebrand Book 6
18th Gone Book 8
19th Firebrand Book 7
20th Gone Book 9
21st Firebrand Book 8
22nd Gone Book 10
23rd Gone Book 11
24th Gone Book 12
25th Gone Book 13
26th Firebrand Book 9 (End)
27th Gone Book 14
28th Gone Book 15
29th Gone Book 16
30th Gone Book 17
31st Gone Book 18 (End)
32nd Edges Book 5
33rd Edges Book 6
34th Edges Book 7
35th Edges Book 8
36th Edges Book 9 (End)

Main Characters

- **Sarah Paradise** - School Teacher
- **Bjorn Esterday** - Reporter at the Daily Memo Newspaper. Works for Sammy Scribe.
- **Percy Snatcher** - Head of the AnCor cell
- **Slash** - Loyal AnCor follower of Percy
- **Noah Lantz** - Earth Farmer husband to Ruth Lantz
- **Joshua Lantz** - Earth Farmer child of Ruth and Noah Lantz
- **Ruth Lantz** - Earth Farmer Mother to Joshua. Wife to Noah. Expert quilter.
- **Jack Courtly** - Head of Courtly City
- **Queenie Courtly** -Wife to Jack Courtly
- **Ace Courtly** - Child of Jack and Queenie Courtly
- **Skipper Courtly** - Brother to Jack Courtly
- **Pip Courtly** - Child of Skipper Courtly
- **Widow Medicina**- Courtly City citizen and train passenger, recently widowed.
- **Mrs Libris** - Librarian

CONTENTS

ACKNOWLEDGMENTS

To all those gentle souls who have graciously given tokens of love, hope, and kind considerations to others.

0 Preface

How does a person believe the unbelievable?

This story is a tangle of revenge and redemption. It is the fervent hunt for love with the sting of loss. It's how myth and illusion take an ordinary school teacher and catapult her into extraordinary circumstances, forcing her to trust what she cannot explain and live in the pursuit of truth.

When she collides with the laser sharp skills of a dashing investigative reporter, her heart races, but can he really be trusted?

How far should she go to verify the facts, to uncover the veracity of the entire story?

Can heart thumping mystery force blind love to triumph despite the odds. The key to the future will only be found in the past as one discovers how to embrace destiny.

When corporations own the justice system, it's dangerous to look for the truth.

1 CHAPTER Year 2030: Sarah, Bus Stop, Library Card, and the ACA (Continuous Ch 01)

Sarah Paradise stood at the bus stop carefully examining an antique Library card, when a booming Soldier Police alert blasted through the electromagnetic audio mass communication broadcast system:

"ACA spotted outside of town! All wheeled vehicles will now evacuate all roads immediately." The Anti-Corporate Activity warning reverberated through the streets echoing repeatedly.

1

Her approaching bus halted. Its passengers promptly disembarked and rushed away leaving the area deserted. The empty bus silently drove off, disappearing into thick fog.

"Not another ACA," Sarah groaned as she quickly unzipped her back pack, and tucked away the treasured Library card into a hidden pocket. She took off her work pumps and pushed them inside the backpack, as well. Before zipping her pack shut, she pulled out old worn Courtly Corporation running shoes and slipped them on. Without the bus, she knew it would be a long exhausting sweaty run to the railway station.

She smoothed her hair back, attempting to look presentable. She was determined to keep her promise to the Kindergarteners who had been waiting excitedly for this field trip to Library.

Her breathing paced with the squeaks of her rubber soles slapping against the sidewalk. She felt the heels of her work shoes jabbing through her backpack every time her foot struck the ground.

The mist was heavy against her face as drops of sweat trickled down her back.

She still wondered why the Administrators had reacted the way they did to the history lessons Sarah Paradise had shared with her class. About life in the city. A long time ago. Before there were "ACAs".

The kids loved those lessons.

She had augmented the minimal school-approved content with facts she had discovered in Library. She suspected that was the real reason the Administrators had reduced her already rationed credits. Her diminished salary pinched her tiny budget and forced her to move into an even smaller apartment... but then you never know what the Administrators are really thinking.

She simply had to gracefully adapt to the fact that she could no longer afford any communication devices... at least for the time being.

Finally, the train station loomed

ahead. She had to stop running and take forced deep breaths of soot-filled fog as she rested her hands on her knees. Wiping sweat from her forehead, she squinted into the sky to peer at hot air balloons drifting to their destinations.

Taking in a last deep breath, Sarah Paradise sprinted with all her might toward the train station.

Swarms of people glutted the once grand, now dilapidated, entrance. The ebb and flow of the oblivious wealthy avoiding the despised poor blocked Sarah's path to the entrance.

Today, the train station crowds seemed different somehow. Were there more Soldier Police than usual? Instinctively, she patted the hiding place of Library card so that it would not be confiscated.

2 CHAPTER Year 2030: Train Station-Bad Kill, Slash (Continuous Ch 02)

Percy Snatcher hissed. "That was a bad kill, Slash. It took too long for him to die." He rushed to peel the uniform off the dead porter's body.

Amidst the sea of wealthy corporate passengers inside the station, the rebel AnCors, or "Anti-Corporatists", Percy Snatcher and Slash were trying to blend in.

Percy Snatcher, the smaller of the two, yanked on the tiny uniform of the now dead porter. Slash bent down to pick up the metal case he was assigned to carry.

5

They tried to fold the porter's short, stout, underwear-clad corpse behind a stack of suitcases and trunks in the luggage bay.

The dead porter's trouser hem hovered just above Percy Snatcher's ankles. The jacket sleeves floated somewhere between his elbow and wrist. Percy Snatcher snapped a bungee cord off a nearby suit case and tied it around his waist. It had to do. It had to work.

Percy Snatcher said. "They won't find the body in this busy crowd. Let's go... You have to get yourself a uniform, too. Avoid suspicion." Percy wrinkled his nose at Slash.

"Keep distance?" Slash offered.

"Good idea." Percy nodded as he tried to adjust his pant waist so his uniform wouldn't slide off. "Talk only when necessary."

A squeal of breaks made Slash jump back. The luxury train bearing the "Courtly Dynamics Corporation" logo roared into the station. Doors swished open.   Out streamed uniformed Soldier Police employed by the mega-company. They raced like ants from an anthill that had just been kicked.   Following, came the wealthy executives dripping in smug attitude, arrogantly unaware of servants in uniform, especially a porter's uniform.

Slash nervously clutched the handle of the metal case and frowned at the oncoming Soldier Police.

"Don't worry, Slash," Percy whispered, "when you get a uniform, you'll be invisible, too."   Percy kept the momentum going as they both fought the crowds disembarking. They had a target to find and couldn't afford to get swept back by the masses. They both were desperate to get on board that train fast.

3 CHAPTER Year 2030: Percy Gets Jack's Photo (Continuous Ch 03)

As they pushed through the crowd, Slash surreptitiously showed Percy Snatcher a crumpled photograph ripped from an old newspaper.

Slash peered at the image of a confident Jack Courtly posing with Earth Farmers.

"I got you a picture so you know him this time. You know, to help you with remembering faces." Slash commented, "Hey. What is cheo?"

"It means C.E.O. Jack Courtly is the

Chief Executive Officer. He runs the corporation!" Percy snapped.

The picture was captioned "CEO Jack Courtly Announces Alliance with Earth Farmers".

"Don't wave that thing around!" Percy ordered glancing up at Slash, "You know they'd kill you if they found you with that picture."

Slash, clearly frightened, looked down at Percy as he shoved the crumpled sweaty photo into Percy's jacket pocket.

Impatient, Percy snapped, "All right. All right! I'll keep it."

Percy Snatcher continued, "If you don't get a uniform, you'll have to stay on the platform. We lost valuable manpower at the check point, but I need you on that train to get this job done."

Slash avoided looking at the shiny dark visors covering all Soldier Police eyes. He simply looked away from them. He tried to draw in his gangly body, hoping his shabby civilian clothes wouldn't be noticed.

Slash hoarsely spoke while his stomach rumbled, "Do we have to do this now? I'm hungry."

Percy stopped mid-stride and glared at Slash, "Listen! I know that we AnCors have no food. We have no care for our wounded. Nowhere to call home. I know that those greedy rich will never be satisfied until they take everything from us, who have nothing. I know our most ambitious AnCor member longs to sleep in a clean bed...but we cannot change anything...Unless we quietly stick to the plan. Understand?"

Slash nodded, eagerly smiling, exposing missing teeth. "Who will take his place when he leaves?" Slash asked looking past Percy's shoulder.

Slowly, Percy turned to follow Slash's gaze. Not twenty feet away stood the man in the picture. Or was it? Was it really their target?

Percy couldn't risk looking at the photo in his pocket with all these people around. Percy was uncertain. He always had trouble recognizing faces. This time should he trust a fool like Slash to identify the target?

4 CHAPTER Year 2030: Encounter Between Jack and Skip (Continuous Ch 04)

As porters helped elegant passengers to get on board, Jack Courtly, the hands-on president of Courtly Dynamics Corporation, turned frustrated to face Skipper Jack, his younger brother, standing beside him, tall, indifferent. His conventionally cut chestnut hair framed his square-jawed face. Clearly, Jack was the more athletically disciplined of the two brothers from his competitive fencing and pony polo

12

matches, and years of serious training in hand-to-hand combative arts.

On the other hand, Skipper the eldest brother, would never engage in such exhausting encounters. Rather, he devoted his attention to fashion and parties. Skipper, always the foppish figurehead, smiled unperturbed from his soft pudding-like face, adjusting his glasses with a pudgy finger.

Behind them, two adolescent youths were playing roughly on the platform while their fathers, the Courtly brothers, ignored them.

Slash and Percy stepped in to eavesdrop.

The elder boy grabbed his cousin's designer jacket collar, trying to remove it.

"Get Uncle Skipper to buy you your own, Pip!" Snarled Ace, defiant 12 year old.

"Why buy later what I can take now? And, Ace, your jacket will fit me," the cousin taunted.

Ace deftly wiggled out of Pip's grasp while straightening the crumpled jacket, and sneering at Pip.

Ace's mother, Queenie, searched her handbag for a lipstick. Worry evaporated from the elegant woman's knitted brow once the slender AromaX brand tube was in her grasp. One usually mustn't apply cosmetics in public, but she was "roughing it". She smiled guiltily as the creamy substance moistened her glistening lips. Yes, she was rebelliously applying lipstick in the thick of a crowd.

Was Ace saying something, Queenie wondered? Then dismissed the feeling as she pressed her lips together and triumphantly popped the beautifying tube into her expensive purse.

Percy wondered if this was the Courtly family, why are they not on the train? Which was the target? The taller one or the shorter one? Percy had to think and secretly look at that picture again. He hated being bad at recognizing faces. He once was told he had a mild case of prosopagnosia, but had never been tested by a doctor.

Quickly, Percy walked away to think. He was excellent at strategic planning. He just needed a moment to decide his next move. Percy assumed Slash would follow obediently.

Noticing Percy's sudden departure, Slash raced after him unknowingly kicking over an Earth Farmer's sewing bag. Spools of thread rolled out onto the ground. Slash kicked the spools away, ignoring this peasant woman. After all, he almost tripped on them.

"Bad Earthie!" Slash cracked as he trailed behind Percy.

Ruth Lantz, simple Earth Farmer woman, kneeled to quickly scoop up the rolling spools of thread. Ruth Lantz was familiar with his kind. Those AnCors always felt entitled, justified, and had a flexible definition of right and wrong. But, forgiveness and patience are due to all men. Even the rude ones who do not respect the God-fearing old ways; those who blindly damage, yet refuse to repair. No. No. Ruth Lantz, devoted Earth

15

Farmer mother and wife, admonished herself for thinking such cross thoughts. Forgiveness and patience are due to all men. She took a deep breath. That meant all of them.

Joshua, eyes politely downcast as Earth Farmer children were trained to do, hurried to his mother's aid, helping her quickly repack her sewing bag. They scurried off to board the third-class car. The train sounded its nearing departure.

"Mother, father will join us soon, but the ticket man is still explaining how the floating image tickets work. We are to meet him at the door of the train and we must all board together."

"Yes, Joshua. You are a good son to convey this message." Mrs. Ruth Lantz clutched her son's arm with one hand and her sewing bag with the other as mother and son wended their way through the crowd.

On the platform, outside the Courtly Private car, Jack Courtly looked challengingly into his brother Skipper's eyes and warned, "I asked you to take this one, Skip, but you refused. So, now I've got a train to catch."

"Hey, Jack, stop worrying. As your elder brother, I was supposed to take over the company when Dad retired, but I'm OK with him going against all tradition and making my YOUNGER brother – you- in charge. Look, you've been working hard and Queenie...I mean what a wife you've got... she must be exhausted decorating your vacation homes. Don't worry. Trust me. I'll keep things going while you enjoy this well-deserved vacation. Just board that train before we need to separate our kids." Skipper physically pushed Ace toward Jack and took his son Pip by the shoulder to stand next to him.

Queenie, the svelte quietly elegant wife of Jack, cooed, "Shall we board, now, Jack, Darling? Ace, come along, Daddy and I are ready to get settled in... Stop teasing your cousin Pip. His father has to take him to the office, now, Ace. Oh, Porter...Porter... our luggage, please."

Having lost sight of Percy, Slash

decided to proceed with the plan himself. Forgetting that he was not yet wearing a porter's uniform, he pushed another approaching porter out of the way and was about to reach for the Courtly trunks and hatboxes, while still clinging to his small metal case.

Suddenly, the chief porter gripped Slash's arm, pulling him aside. With a snap of his fingers, the chief porter assigned a properly uniformed employee to help continue moving the luggage down the aisle into the correct cabin.

The Courtly family, already on the train, never noticed the commotion occurring behind them.

Admonishing him, the Chief porter started to scold Slash, "Young man. Just because the ACA forces every citizen to the train station does not mean you can board a car meant for the upper classes. This area is restricted. It is not for the likes of you."

Curious, 12-year-old Ace briefly turned back to investigate what was going on.

5 CHAPTER- Year 2030: Slash Attacks the Conductor (Continuous Ch 05)

Unable to really see anything, Ace shrugged, turned away, and ran to catch up with the Courtly family just as the porter paraded the wealthy group into their private car.

Brass sconces filled with fresh sweet smelling flowers adorned the inlaid burled wood walls. Plush leather cushioned seats and velvet curtains gave it a charm that made one feel transported to a magical place. The décor

19

was consistent with Mr. Courtly's requirements for a family vacation of peace, comfort, and one free from technical distractions.

Servants deftly unpacked the bags and hung garments properly. Mrs. Courtly indicated to her husband that she was pleased.

Mr. Courtly thanked the workers with a smile and healthy tip, which was received most appreciatively.

Ace, bored already, flopped down on an overstuffed cushion and stared out the window.

Just outside the train car, the stern Chief porter refused to loosen his grip on Slash's upper arm, wincing at Slash's foul breath. Slash struck the chief porter with the metal case he was holding, stunning the Chief porter. He jerked himself free and ran. Quickly, Slash got lost among the milling crowds on the platform. Slash's heart pounded painfully. His mouth went dry.

The Chief porter, regaining his senses,

fumbled for his communicator and shouted into it.

Slash searched for his leader, Percy. This was not part of the plan. Slash had wanted to make Percy proud and have something to brag about back at camp. Terrified, Slash realized the SPs were everywhere, closing in on him. He couldn't see Percy anywhere.

What had Slash just done?

Slash remembered his indoctrination. The wealthy never notice the invisible servant class. That's why servants make the best cover identities for AnCors. But, here Slash felt very exposed and not invisible at all.

The SPs were walking toward him, now.

Slash couldn't see their eyes because of the visors they wore, but their noses were all pointed right at him.

With efficient organization, Soldier Police were already forming a human barrier of emotionless authority, sealing off Percy's access to the train like an impenetrable wall. The SPs scrutinized every person within sight.

Another unit of SPs moved to block all possible escape routes from within the train station. Windows, doors, tunnels, and servant's entrances were to be electronically barricaded.

Outside on the street, Sarah Paradise and the large crowd of pedestrians had been kept from entering the train station by a stolid wall of soldiers.

"Oh," she groaned in her thoughts, "another search". She started to slip her backpack off, making sure the Library card was still hidden from view.

A stern Soldier Police stood in her path preventing her from entering the train station. Sarah saw other SPs pushing back the incoming public. She looked quizzically at the SP who had stopped her.

"Ma'am, we have a situation and are sealing off the station while we investigate. You are not allowed in." Other SPs gave the same message to everyone else trying to gain entry.

At first, Sarah didn't know how to respond. Situation? What situation would warrant shoving the public away from the train station during an ACA?

"I have a ticket."

Sarah waved to get the attention of the Soldier Police, again. She tapped a button on her school-branded unit which suddenly produced a floating holographic image of a third class ticket with a countdown to when the train would depart.

Urgently, Sarah exclaimed, "I only have a few minutes to board and you are keeping us all outside the station!"

"Your school is authorized to receive a full refund which can be applied to another ticket for another day. Please keep back. No one is allowed in to the station." He continued to program the electronic barricade.

"I have no violations. I'm a safe passenger. See?" Quickly, Sarah searched for the fob she wore at her hip. The SP's eyes were blocked by the dark visor, which served as a screen for the Soldier Police to read messages and search information. She could not see his expression.

Sarah waved at him. Her HIB, Holographic Identification Badge, fob dangled like an ornamental jewel on her belt, but she quickly plucked it off and handed it to the officer, who coldly made contact with Miss Paradise, again.

He took the bauble and slipped it into his sleeve in an indentation labeled "HIB". A transparent image of Sarah appeared on the officer's eye visor, which only he could read.

He spoke aloud, "Name: Sarah Paradise. Occupation: Teacher. Behavior record: Clean-No Offenses. Yes. Teacher Paradise, your identity has been confirmed."

"Good. And you see, I've got twenty little kids waiting for me to lead them on a field trip. I really need to be there for them."

"Sorry, Teacher Paradise. You'll have to contact your School Administration on your communication device to reschedule." He efficiently handed back her HIB fob.

"On my salary, I can't afford any communication devices. Do you understand? Sir?" Sarah clipped the fob back on her belt as he turned away.

She interrupted his programming of the barrier to get his attention again, holding the unit displaying her holographic ticket as she continued, "I do NOT own any communication devices. I DO have a valid ticket. Paid for by the school to allow me, a teacher for the school, to do my job and lead a field trip of students, who attend the school. Understand? It's my job. I have no way to notify them that I cannot meet them. Please let me on that train...I can just catch it!"

She grasped the unit projecting her ticket and pointed to the corner which showed the countdown-to-departure. Time was running out.

The Soldier Police stopped what he was doing and simply looked at the holographic ticket. 10, 9, 8... Then he patiently smiled, "I don't think you can catch your train now, Teacher Paradise. Please step back, in the interest of public safety."

"You can't shut the public out during an ACA, Sir," Sarah protested in vain.

During an ACA, "Anti-Corporate-Activity" Alerts, citizens were prohibited from being inside wheeled vehicles on roads. These rules did not apply to Soldier Police. Train stations were supposed to be neutral territory, allowing for equal treatment of all classes, but it never quite worked that way. During an ACA, trains were one approved alternate transportation that citizens could use.

She realized the futility of arguing. The sea of faces pressed in on her from all sides. She felt thwarted and helpless.

Resigned, she turned toward the streets when she stepped into an aggressively approaching athletic man, pushing his tall frame through the crowds. Her nose bounced right off his well-muscled chest and she stepped back startled. Her instinctive apologies were drowned out by the protesting crowds questioning the barricade.

This man's commanding voice got the immediate attention of the same SP Sarah had just finished speaking to. The Soldier Police paused setting up his barricade and held out an open palm demanding an identification fob, which the man produced immediately.

After clicking the fob into his HIB indentation on his sleeve, the Soldier Police started reviewing the data on his eye visor, which covered his eyes so the public couldn't see where an officer was looking.

"Officer, I work for 'The Daily Memo' and the office scanner heard that a barricade was being set up. What's the story? As a reporter, I request entrance past this barricade to speak to the guy in charge."

The officer spoke into his communication device, while reviewing the holographic identification badge.

"Name: Bjorn Esterday. Occupation: Reporter. Behavior record: Clean-No Offenses. You do not have a ticket to board any train today. Is that correct?" The SP cocked his head as if receiving a reply to his earlier communication. He returned the HIB fob.

"Correct, Sir. May I pass?"

He politely, yet firmly stated, "Reporter Esterday, your request for access has been denied. No civilians. No exceptions. Please step away for your own safety."

The Soldier Police pressed a button and an electronic wall sealed off the first entrance to the station with a low pitched harmonic hum. This was followed sequentially until every entrance to the station had been sealed.

Nobody inside the station could get out and nobody outside, including Sarah, could get in.

An eager member of the crowd pushed toward one barrier with arm outstretched. As soon as his palm touched the force field, he recoiled from the searing pain. Bystanders pulled him back a safe distance and tended to his blistering hand.

The Soldier Police on the other side of the barrier just shook his head and turned away. There was always some fool who was compelled to rush these blockades. They never learned that only the uniforms of the Soldier Police allowed them to safely pass in and out of the barrier.

The force field was meant to keep out the common people. People like Sarah Paradise, earnest school teacher and Bjorn Esterday, dismissed reporter.

"How am I going to get out of here?" Sarah said to herself, "What will happen to the kids?"

6 CHAPTER Year 2030:
Sarah Meets Bjorn During ACA
(Continuous Ch 06)

Outside the building, concentric circles of citizens formed a ring around the station perimeter. At the center were the despondent frustrated people who tried to bribe or threaten their way into the station. These were people who had deadlines, appointments, and no alternate transportation. Their pleas fell onto the deaf ears of the Soldier Police.

Just outside the center were the hopeful ones who wanted to be nearby when the barricade was removed. These were more patient people, willing to wait untold hours just to ensure a good place in line.

On the outer rim were those passengers who simply accepted what appeared to be a capricious closure.

These people drifted about loosely. Some clustered in groups. Some wandered off to nearby hydration stations to socialize. Some walked back home accepting their fate. Others complained to anybody who would listen about feeling helpless in influencing –or even being informed about –a Soldier Police action.

Bjorn pushed through the multitudes like a jet cutting through air. Sarah was happy to take advantage of this man's imposing stature. She hurriedly rode in the wake of the slipstream he created to navigate through the pressing sea of people so she could more easily get away from the crowds around the station.

"I got locked out?" Bjorn stated out loud to himself.

"We both got locked out," Sarah jumped in.

Bjorn spun around realizing he was being followed, then smiled unconsciously as he was greeted with the pleasant unexpected sight of this flustered school teacher.

"Oh?" was all he could say in reply.

"You know how they are. This 'incident' is probably some executive getting claustrophobia...or having a bad hair day and doesn't want the masses to see an embarrassing coiffure, so 'everybody out'."

"'Coiffure'? Not 'hair style?'" He smiled bemusedly.

"Hello? I'm a school teacher," Sarah retorted.

"Maybe you are right," replied Bjorn. "There are good stories out there, but my editor is always worried about legal backlash, so what makes it to print is usually watered down. But, I still have this tendency to dig. I am hopeful that there are some stories out there people would care about if they knew what was happening."

"Well, you didn't get a train station story today. Now what?" Sarah quipped.

"I'll get back to the office and see where the scanner alert sends me."

"Sends you? You mean you'd go to another location in the city from this scanner alert thing?"

"Yes."

"Well, I thought the news business offices are way over on the other side of town..." Sarah squinted her eyes, examining him.

"Yes..." Bjorn smiled, enjoying this conversation.

"Well, how did you get to the station so quickly during an ACA?"

"Horseback."

"Oh? I thought only Earth Farmers use horses."

"Courtly Corp," Bjorn explained, "just started making business arrangements with Earth Farmers, who now have protected status like an endangered species. Because Jack Courtly pioneered a precedent, my boss followed the Courtly Corp example and made a similar arrangement on his own, which means my newspaper now has access to horses like that one over there. See? That's my ride today."

Bjorn pointed toward a tethered horse.

"You ride without a saddle? Just a blanket-mat thing?"

"Yes. I take the horse the way the Daily Memo stable gives it to me... and now I'm heading straight back to my office." Bjorn smiled. "Anyway, it was nice plowing through that crowd with you. When I get to my desk, I will get a new location from the scanner for another story, unless my editor calls me first."

Bjorn Esterday, politely bowed, an archaic gesture, turned his powerful shoulders away, and headed down the street toward his mount tethered in the distance.

After about four strides, Sarah called after him.

"Wait! Mr. Reporter man...person...sir" Sarah quickened her pace to catch up to him with her brightest smile. "I have an urgently important question for you..."

7 CHAPTER Year 2030: Body In The Luggage Bay (Continuous Ch 07)

Meanwhile, back inside the train station the threat level suddenly intensified. From the luggage bay, the corpse of a small, heavy-set man, clad only in his underwear, rolled out from behind a suit case.

Like virulent bacteria in a petri dish, the number of Soldier Police instantly multiplied, sealing off the luggage bay.

The attack on the Chief porter by Slash had initiated the train station lock-down in the first place.

Now, this discovery of a corpse elevated the seriousness of the situation. These attacks on railway employees increased the threat levels, confirming AnCor involvement.

Watching from a short distance away, Percy tugged down the sleeves of his tight jacket and adjusted the waist of the porter's ill fitted uniform to make sure he could reach his gun.

From the platform, Percy searched the crowd for Slash.

Where had Slash disappeared to?

Like a robot, an expressionless SP locked on Percy. Methodically, this uniformed menace approached Percy Snatcher, who at this moment wished he could make his short scrawny frame invisible.

8 CHAPTER Year 2030: Ace, Close That Window (Continuous Ch 08)

"Ace, close that window. The train is moving," Jack Courtly ordered as he turned to settle into the overstuffed chair. His briefcase was within reach.

"There was something going on outside. A crowd on the platform, Dad."

"It's nothing. Just people gathering to board a different train, Ace. Now close that window."

Reluctantly, Ace closed the window and slumped into a softly padded leather seat. A long silence followed until Ace piped in with, "Dad, those Earthie guys dress funny."

"They dress simply because it's part of their beliefs. They are Earth Farmers...Please don't be lazy and use that derogatory term."

"What? Earthies?" Ace quipped.

"Yes. Do not say that word. Learn to respect those around you." Jack Courtly shook his head at his only child.

Queenie opened her hand bag as she scooted next to her husband.

"Jack, Dear, speaking of which...You know who I saw aboard this train, Darling? The little Lantz family."

"Now why does that name sound familiar?" Jack's brow furrowed.

"It just so happens," Queenie continued as Ace stared numbly out the window, "Francois said he needed to decorate around a focal point. We decided on hand-made quilts. I collected paint chip samples for color combinations and scouted all the quilt makers until I found the best one... Ruth Lantz."

She checked her husband's face for any sign of recognition. She continued, "Oh, darling, you don't remember, do you? You really should re-introduce yourself. She's using one of my designs. You know something? She might be working on Ace's quilt... We should wander into third class and say hello."

"Wander into third class? Wander? Wander? I'm not wandering to go look at ridiculous quilts that nobody wants? It's so boring...." Ace suddenly began to mutter, arms limp, jaw loose unable to form the words, pretending to snore, then feign sleeping with exaggerated exhales.

"Enough, Ace!" Mr. Jack Courtly ordered bluntly.

Queenie heard a rustling at the door and opened it.

Suddenly the train lurched to a stop.

In the aisle, just outside their cabin, an elderly woman was struggling to twist the lid off her pill bottle as she was jostled by the swaying train. Queenie Courtly, always gracious and willing to offer of her abundance, reached inside their compartment refrigeration unit and daintily picked up a cool bottle of fresh water. She offered it to the distressed woman.

"Might I share some chilled hydration to assist you in swallowing those pills? Once you open the bottle, that is."

Mrs. Courtly spoke with a welcoming tone as she leaned against the door jam, stopping the cabin door from closing all the way.

The train suddenly lurched forward, again, causing the old woman to brace herself against the wall and Queenie to hold firmly onto the door jam.

She smiled as the woman accepted the proffered bottle of liquid.

Behind Queenie, from inside the cabin, Ace asked, "Dad, why do we keep stopping and starting?"

The old woman smiled at the youth's observations and turned her attention to Queenie, "Thank you for the hydration. How Kind. So refreshing. Almost makes taking this dreadful heart medicine worth the trouble."

The plump older woman shook her head as she finally opened the container of pills, popped one in her mouth, and took a long quenching gulp of liquid.

Queenie wanted to model for Ace how a Courtly is obliged to show kindness even to those not part of their inner circle.

"Would you like another hydrator to take with you to your compartment?" Queenie offered, holding out another frosty unopened bottle. "Compliments of Courtly Dynamics Corporation."

"Oh, yes, I recognize you, now, Mrs. Courtly." The widow curtsied. "Thank you, Mrs. Courtly. I will never throw this bottle away. If I may introduce myself, my name is Widow Medicina. I'm on my way to the Widow's Community run by those Earth Farmers....or nuns..."

"Well, I hope you have a pleasant trip, Widow Medicina. The Earth Farmers are one of my favorite charities. Nuns, too!"

The widow commented, "It's been difficult transitioning into widowhood. I must get used to people calling me that, you understand. 'Widow' instead of 'Missus'? Oh. I've lost my way. I can't seem to find a porter. Can you direct me to my cabin?"

Queenie smiled, then stepped back inside to pick up a map of the train cars and handed it to the widow. After looking at the widow's ticket, Queenie directed the older woman by pointing out the car she should go to on the train map. The elderly befuddled woman humbly accepted the map, and then gathered her belongings overwhelmed and effusively appreciative of Queenie's help.

"So many widows, these days, you know." Widow Medicina smiled up at Queenie and then turned and awkwardly wended her way along the aisle of the swaying train car.

9 CHAPTER Year 2030:Horse Ride to Library (Continuous Ch 09)

Sitting behind Bjorn on his horse, Sarah's arms were wrapped tightly around his waist as they trotted toward Library. When they came into view, the children, who were waiting on the front steps, squealed and clapped their hands excitedly, rushing toward them.

Bjorn quickly reined the horse to a stop with a low "whoa" as soon as he saw the children. The Kindergarteners instantly surrounded his horse, clamoring with delight, reaching eagerly to touch the animal.

Some parents, who were watching for the very tardy Miss Paradise, were relieved she had finally arrived. As soon as the adults greeted her, they indicated they had to rush off to their various appointments. They entrusted the group of children to Sarah Paradise's capable hands.

Library doors had not yet quite opened up.

Sarah released her grip from around Bjorn's waist. With one powerful arm, he eased her gently to the ground.

"A little late is better than never arriving, at all," Bjorn smiled.

As Sarah stood on the ground, she secured her backpack on her shoulders, and straightened her knees out of that bow-legged position. She dusted horse hair off as she looked up at the old faded façade of Library.

She didn't need a silly train when reporter Bjorn Esterday galloped her right to the front steps. He never asked Sarah for directions. She wondered how he knew where to find the building when so many people didn't even know Library was still opened to the public.

"I really appreciate it, Mr. Esterday," Sarah smiled as the small children excitedly surrounded her. "Dropping me off here was very kind of you. I honestly didn't think you'd agree to my silly request. Hope I didn't make you late for anything."

"I need to head back to my office and pick up another assignment. I promised my boss I'd get some kind of a story today," he smiled.

"Yes. It is important to keep your word. To adults and to children. You helped me keep a promise to these children. Thank you."

She didn't know what else to say as she looked up into his eyes. He seemed even more handsome as the sun's rays formed a halo around his head.

His demeanor was proper and well-mannered. Had he always been a reporter or did he have some military training? She wondered how this man came to be the person he was today: considerate, knowledgeable, gallant, and obviously disciplined enough to exercise regularly. He just didn't fit the image of a scruffy gruff reporter.

Bjorn remained mounted, but leaned down to whisper to Sarah,

"I secretly love..." he paused to adjust the reins, "...Library, also."

"Oh, so that's how you knew where it was! You've been here before. Do you know where our School Kindergarten is?"

"Only if I was invited to locate it," he winked.

"It's just two blocks that way," she laughed, pointing.

He noticed the children staring up at him.

"So, anyway," Bjorn nodded toward the building just behind them, "your kids are obviously excited about all the facts they'll find in Library, Miss Paradise. I'm sure it will be an adventure for them."

Bjorn straighten up as his communication device rapidly flashed. "It's my boss. He's sending me to some location to cover another story. But may we..." he turned his mount around carefully to avoid frightening the children, "...may I communicate with you, later, Miss Paradise?"

"Oh." Sarah looked down at the ground. She was still wearing her Courtly Corp running shoes and felt very unprepared for a romantic overture.

"Well, it's just that I don't have any communication devices, Mr. Esterday."

Bjorn gave a polite nod, abruptly pressed his heels to the sides of the horse, and trotted off.

The children waved goodbye.

As he disappeared down the road, Sarah Paradise wondered if she would ever see him again.

10 CHAPTER Year 2030: Sarah's Book Lesson (Continuous Ch 10)

Bjorn's thoughts raced as the horse galloped along. Bjorn could plunge enthusiastically into the most difficult news assignment, but when presented with an attractive woman, who shared a love of books, he was at a loss.

Until he had encountered Sarah, the women he met seemed superficial, as if they were entitled to manipulate circumstances to get as much as they could from anyone. It seemed nobody valued what was right or wrong...only what was convenient.

Here, he was presented with Sarah Paradise, who seemed earnest, genuine, and unaware of a pure beauty shining through her disheveled harried exterior. Her presence made the cautious planner in him freeze up like an awkward glacier. When she rejected his mild overture, he ran.

Literally galloped away.

Why did she have this impact on him? No matter. He had stories to work on. A lot of stories. He wasn't, after all, born yesterday. It was time to move on with the day.

Sarah stood there gazing at the empty lane where Bjorn Esterday had ridden off.

The murmur of the children blended together into an indiscernible soup of high-pitched chatter and squeals.

She hoped Mr. Esterday didn't think she was dismissing him. After all, she was telling the truth about not having a communication device. She wasn't trying to avoid giving him her contact information, but just didn't have any to give.

Besides, if he really wanted to see her again, he knew where the Kindergarten was. He could come by her work place, if he so chose. But, he said he'd only come if invited, and she didn't know how to invite him. Sarah thought his departure was rather abrupt. And now he was gone.

What an odd day this was turning out to be, she thought.

As if waking up from a trance, Sarah finally realized the children had circled around her, tugging on her hands and clothes to get her attention. They had spotted the librarian unlocking the front doors to Library. They'd be the first ones in, they squealed to each other.

Sarah figured they'd probably be the only ones in for the whole day, if not the entire month. People had forgotten how valuable Library was. The only reason this establishment was still free to the public was due to some odd clause in an eccentric rich man's will that said it must stay opened to the public for something like another hundred years.

"Yes, class," Sarah said looking directly into their excited eyes. It was better that she stay focused on work.

"Before we walk into Library, I have something special to show you." She carefully slipped off her backpack, opened a pocket inside and took out the Library card.

The children gasped. One child waved his hand over it perplexed as to why no holographic image appeared. Another child also tried, with no results.

"What does it do, Miss Paradise? It is not morphing," the child asked waving his hands in a manner that would evoke a holographic image in other card-sized devices.

"There is no image that appears. This is a very old card that gave permission to any citizen to find out information about any subject..."

The children clamored around to see this powerful card which appeared to lack functionality, perplexed as to how a static piece of paper could be so powerful.

"How does it do that? It just sits there."

Each child held out one finger, as Sarah had taught them, to use their "gentle hands" to touch the card. Sarah stood in front so they all got the opportunity to tap on it.

"You remember our discussion on books, right, class? They have pages and we use one finger to press down on the right side and swipe to the left."

She demonstrated by swiping her right index finger to the left. The class mimicked her actions.

She continued, "On the other side of the page is more information we can read, starting from the top left.

Remember our lesson on numbers? Even numbers are on the left pages. Odd numbers are on the right pages. By using this Library card, you could take these books out of the building of Library and bring them into your own home."

"So Library would give people gifts?" one child piped up.

"Well, by showing this card to a librarian, you promised Library to bring the books back when you were done looking at them," Sarah explained.

"Isn't it rude to give a gift back to the giver?"

"Well, it is not a 'gift', but a 'loan'. When you are done borrowing the book, you return it so another citizen child, like yourself, will be able to read the same things. This land has a history of sharing knowledge freely with each other." Sarah took a breath. "Fun knowledge like fairy tales. Fact knowledge like how to build or fix things. Knowledge sharing made our ancestors a strong population. They could efficiently research facts and then apply those facts to fix problems by themselves." Sarah paused to make sure she still held their attention

"Our ancestors could verify what an authority figure told them by checking the facts to see if it was true. So, it was harder to fool them."

"So they has less problems than we do?" The children were transfixed, pondering these revelations.

"They had fewer problems," Sarah gently corrected. "Our ancestors were not smarter, but they could go to Library to get the facts. Now, are we ready to go inside and meet the librarian, Mrs. Libris?"

Inside, Sarah smiled as the children gazed around, rendered speechless, overwhelmed by the sight of rows of bookshelves crammed with printed knowledge.

"I'd like to introduce you to Mrs. Libris, the librarian. She is going to explain how this place works," Sarah whispered.

Mrs. Libris pointed to a sign on the wall and asked the children if they could read it.

It read: ***ipsa scientia potestas est***.

"It is in a different language," Mrs. Libris carefully explained.

"Like a code?" one of the group asked enthusiastically.

"Yes," Mrs. Libris smiled. She continued, "the code is called 'Latin' and it was quoted by a man in 1597. His name was Francis Bacon. Do you know what it means?"

The children all whispered that they did not know what it meant. One child offered that the man, Mr. Bacon, must be very old by now.

"It means 'knowledge itself is power'. So,

here in Library, you can find that knowledge. Facts and such. That gives you, children, the authority – or power- to know what is true. This is why your teacher, Miss Paradise, asks you to do homework. So you can learn and grow up to become powerful, honest, honorable citizens armed with the truth."

One precocious child asked in a loud whisper, "What stuff can you learn from those books?"

Mrs. Libris paused and answered, "Do you know that your very own teacher, Miss Paradise, used to come here to read all sorts of books. She studied old manuals. She even built a real working antique computer from scratch, which we have over there in our history section. Would you like to see it?"

The children, wide-eyed, all whispered, "Yes". Mrs. Libris beckoned them to follow her.

Sarah smiled as she stepped away, letting the librarian continue her supportive lecture.

This is turning out to be a good day, after all, thought Sarah. She imagined herself as a mamma goose with her fluffy goslings happily playing.

This moment was made possible by Bjorn, a man who was kind, strong, gentlemanly, and handsome; a man she might never see again.

Behind her, Sarah heard the rapid footsteps of an out-of-breath coworker, who had obviously chased her down.

"Miss Paradise, Miss Paradise!" The woman waved.

"What is it?" Sarah asked, as she stepped away from the children so Mrs. Libris, the librarian, could continue her tour.

"The Administrators. They just changed your status from Kindergarten to Secondary High. I'm so sorry to give you yet another message from them, but you need to head back to the school. You need to report to the High School campus across town tomorrow." The messenger spoke, trying to catch her breath.

The woman produced a tablet, touched a button and showed it to Sarah. Sarah glanced at the children, who were walking away with Mrs. Libris. They were very happily occupied.

Sarah turned back to this messenger of doom. Orders confirmed. She no longer was a teacher at the Kindergarten campus and had to report to a totally different part of town.

"I have documented parental consent for this trip, today. The school approved a train ticket for me to get here. I don't understand what the problem is or why they would switch me so suddenly."

The woman felt for Miss Paradise, a good instructor who always bonded with the children in her class. This messenger struggled for a moment to decide if she should tell this teacher the real story.

"Miss Paradise, the official reason for this change is to ensure your teaching capabilities are well-rounded and applicable for all ages to better serve the corporation's program of continuous teacher improvement."

"What is the real reason? Please?"

The woman leaned in whispering, guiding Sarah a few steps away for privacy.

"In a meeting, I overheard them saying they suspect you might be planting anti-corporate ideas in impressionable minds. They thought that by reclassifying you with older children, you would have less influence on them. Older children never listen to adults, right? They figure you'll stop telling those memorable fables."

"Memorable fables? You mean history lessons? Look, these are small children. They'll probably forget everything I teach them, anyway. So what does it matter?"

The messenger nodded sympathetically, and whispered, "Miss Paradise, even I remember the things you've shared and I only stopped by your classroom every now and then to drop off papers."

"Really?" Sarah folded her arms, feeling foiled. "What do you remember?"

The woman cleared her throat as she tried to prove her point, "A long time ago, citizens..." She cleared her throat again and continued, "...Fire elimination services were offered for any structure found ablaze-no membership in a fire prevention club was required. Education was offered to all children of the public, regardless of class and income. Potable water was freely accessible through faucets in any home. Written documents could be delivered by a large nation-wide institution called...what was it...Pre Office?"

"It was called a Post Office," Sarah corrected without realizing it.

"Right, Miss. Paradise. A 'Post Office!' And any citizen of any age could buy a picture to affix on the document's outer shell...a 'stamp', which proved you willingly donated to the salaries of those who delivered your package to wherever you wanted it sent... I mean need I go on?"

"No. I just didn't realize..." Sarah's voice faded.

"No. Miss Paradise, I know you don't realize the insane fantasies that tumble out of your mouth. Listen. A re-classification is much better than another reduction in your credits, right?" She smiled kindly, trying to comfort Sarah Paradise.

"But, how can telling the truth be viewed so antagonistically?" Sarah wondered out loud.

"Miss Paradise. I am a supporter of creative thought, but you asked 'why' and if I may be candid, I must tell you that these stories make you sound a little off-center. Especially when you act as if these are historical facts. You know those fables are not in any of our approved school information resources."

She searched Sarah's face for a reaction. Sarah just looked at the ground with her arms folded.

"Miss Paradise, I've got to get back to the school. I feel so badly that I had to bring you this news. Stop your field trip now and walk the children back to class or the Administrators may authorize another salary reduction...but the choice is yours..." The woman hesitated, then hurried off.

Sarah stood there looking at the little children enraptured with the sweeping arm gestures of Mrs. Libris, the old librarian.

"Well, do I bring them back, realizing they will never have this opportunity again? Or do I let them stay and risk my job?"

She suddenly remembered that her good shoes were still in her back pack. She had wanted to wear them for this special trip to Library. She looked at the departing messenger, then back at the children.

She unzipped her back pack, took off her Courtly Corp running shoes, slipped on her polished 'special occasion shoes', then walked toward the children.

11 CHAPTER Year 2030: Slash And The Soldier Police   (Continuous Ch 11)

Slash, on the train platform, searched for a way to dodge the Soldier Police slowly approaching him.

From the platform, Slash searched the train windows hoping for some sign of Percy, but he didn't appear to be on board. He should have been on the train by now. Wasn't Percy following his own time table?

The train suddenly started to move, then lurched to a stop.

Slash exhaled. He was getting a headache. Slash, gripping the case more tightly, looked around desperately for his companion. With Percy nowhere in sight, Slash decided he had to be a man of action and move the plan forward himself.

Percy will need this case to complete the job and he would hand it to Percy as soon as he found him. Oh, Percy would be so thankful to Slash. Maybe even compliment him. But they were supposed to do this assignment together as a team.

Slash smiled to himself. His own quick thinking would make a good story for the other AnCors back at camp.

Realizing that the train was at a stop, Percy, not able to find Slash, assumed his comrade must already be on board. Percy bolted for the train caboose, heaved himself over the caboose rail pulling himself onboard, unaware that Slash was still on the platform.

Percy's reach had caused the small porter jacket to rip. Once aboard, he knew he couldn't wear a ripped uniform. All that effort to get it, and now it was useless. He'd have to improvise.

Abruptly, the train lurched forward, again. It whistled as it started, picking up speed.

Percy pulled the jacket off, throwing it onto the tracks, hoping he could now just blend into third class. He adjusted the bungee cord holding up his pant waist to make sure the gun didn't drop out.

It was still there.

He walked quickly down the long aisle of the third class cars, where Slash and he were supposed to meet if they got separated. He hurried through one car after another. His pace quickened as he searched for Slash.

Slash was not on board the train.

Where was he?

12 CHAPTER Year 2030: The Metal Case Flies (Continuous Ch 12)

Percy anxiously peered out through a caboose window at the retreating platform, frustrated.

The train kept moving in starts and stops.

Security was getting tighter with each passing minute.

There he was! Percy saw Slash was still on the platform!

How could Slash still be on the platform? He knew the time table.

It got worse.

Slash was holding the metal case that Percy needed urgently to carry out his mission. Percy needed the case more than he needed Slash.

Percy stepped outside onto the caboose landing and waved to get Slash's attention, but to no avail.

After all the rehearsals, how could this have happened?

The train picked up speed.

Slash, bewildered, became engulfed in the crowd of people producing their HIBs. The wave of Soldier Police methodically pushed through the crowds, clicking HIBs into their sleeve indentations, questioning various individuals.

Horrified, Percy helplessly witnessed Slash suddenly break into a run parallel to the train backtracking toward the caboose. Soldier Police gave chase, closing in on Slash like a hangman's noose.

From his position on the caboose, Percy helplessly watched Slash trying to race toward him.

Slash saw Percy leaning against the caboose railing and with one desperate heave, flung the case toward the retreating train. Percy gripped the railing with one hand and reached out, straining to catch the metal case in mid-air.

Barely missing its mark, the tin valise clattered on the opposing tracks, spilling its mechanical contents and drug filled syringes across the creosote soaked grade 5 wooden railroad ties. An approaching train suddenly whooshed by on those tracks as it was pulling into the station, causing a gust of air to knock Percy off his feet as the train passed.

The contents of the metal case were instantly pulverized and made useless. The SP now caught up to Slash.

Frustrated, Percy groaned as he closed his eyes. All that planning! All the drills and practice! For nothing!

"Now, I have to improvise," Percy muttered as he turned his back on Slash, abandoning him to his fate at the hands of the Soldier Police. Percy ducked back inside the shelter of the caboose. He wasn't about to risk himself and the operation to help out a fool.

Percy had a schedule to keep. He checked to see if he still had a gun. One gun. How could their plan possibly work, now?

13 CHAPTER- What Will Happen Next?

Bjorn Esterday, reporter, met and assisted Sarah Paradise, teacher, to Library during an ACA. She felt a connection to him as they rode on his Daily Memo newspaper issued steed, but will she ever see him again?

Jack Courtly, the ruler of Courtly City, and his older brother Skipper seem to be at odds. Will they work things out after Jack returns from his vacation with his family, Queenie and Ace?

Now that Sarah taught her students about Library being a place to find facts in old fashioned books with paper pages, will they appreciate the sacrifices Sarah has made for them?

Slash and Percy Snatcher killed a porter for his uniform. Will the SPs get them for the senseless murder?

AnCor Slash seems to be outnumbered by the SPs. Will he reunite with the other AnCors?

Now that the AnCor metal case flew, missing the train, and landing on the tracks, is the original AnCor mission abandoned? What will Percy Snatcher do?

ଓ **To Be Continued...** ଔ

14 Did You Know

Andrew Carnegie (think Carnegie Hall) was a self-taught man. Raised in poverty, died in wealth, his pet project was building libraries between 1882 - 1929, as long as the city agreed to staff and fund it. He donated over $60 million dollars to an effort he said would "bring books and information to all people". This took place right before the Great Depression.

In total, Andrew Carnegie built 2509 Carnegie libraries, 1689 of them in the United States. That means that by 1930 about half of all libraries in the USA were being built by Andrew Carnegie. Think about how many wealthy people today feel obliged to spend that kind of money on educating the general population.

We learn that AnCor, Percy Snatcher, has trouble recognizing faces of people. This is a documented medical condition called Prosopagnosia (Pro- so – PAG- no-jha).   It is from the Greek: "prosopon" = "face", "agnosia" = "not knowing". It is also commonly called "face blindness". People with this condition can recognize other objects but not human faces.

Those affected with it, still have their ability to reason, strategize, and make effective decisions.

The underside of the two lobes in your brain is what seems to be impacted by Prosopagnosia (Pro- so – PAG- no-jha).

The area is called the "Fusiform Gyrus", which facilitates recognition of faces. It was originally thought this syndrome resulted from a physical injury, but researchers now say it can be something you are born with.

This story, EDGES, shows that despite any setback or physical limitation, it is possible to live life, strategize, even be cunning.

In other words, who you are is defined by the decisions you make and how you help or hurt others. 'Who you are' is not determined by any limitation you think has been imposed upon you either physically or by circumstances.

Now, ask yourself this: Have the decisions of others created circumstances which made your life difficult? Has suffering been foisted upon you by events over which you have no control? How will you determine to make those small everyday decisions to do the right thing to show you live a life of integrity and are on the right path? Will you make considerate or selfish choices?

About Wynter Sommers

Wynter Sommers is the pseudonym for an American writing team, which harnesses multiple skills in technology, research, and education. Formally trained with a PhD in Education, Wynter Sommers blends academic classroom experience, with corporate sophistication, and a passion for developing more effective student insights.

Wynter Sommers has taught classrooms of enthusiastic children. She has a heart to inspire creativity and develop critical thinking skills, all to encourage students to make wise choices in life. She wants to impart the talent of honing one's skills in self-reliance and collaborative team work. Despite any environmental barriers outside of an individual's control, Wynter Sommers wishes to impart the message that genuine hope, love, and peace can help us overcome obstacles, and cement friendships. Wynter Sommers hopes you enjoy the other ***Bjorn Esterday Was not Born Yesterday*** stories in this series.

www.ingramcontent.com/pod-product-compliance
Lightning Source LLC
Chambersburg PA
CBHW051841020726
47502CB00005B/1904